DESMOND COLE GHOST PATROL

3 BOOKS IN 1!

THE HAUNTED HOUSE NEXT DOOR
GHOSTS DON'T RIDE BIKES, DO THEY?
SURF'S UP, CREEPY STUFF!

by **Andres Miedoso**
illustrated by **Victor Rivas**

LITTLE SIMON
New York   Amsterdam/Antwerp   London
Toronto   Sydney/Melbourne   New Delhi

If you purchased this book without a cover, you should be aware that this book is stolen property. It was reported as "unsold and destroyed" to the publisher, and neither the author nor the publisher has received any payment for this "stripped book."

This book is a work of fiction. Any references to historical events, real people, or real places are used fictitiously. Other names, characters, places, and events are products of the author's imagination, and any resemblance to actual events or places or persons, living or dead, is entirely coincidental.

LITTLE SIMON
An imprint of Simon & Schuster Children's Publishing Division
1230 Avenue of the Americas, New York, New York 10020
This Little Simon paperback July 2025
The Haunted House Next Door and *Ghost Don't Ride Bikes, Do They?*
© 2017 by Simon & Schuster, LLC.
Surf's Up, Creepy Stuff! © 2018 by Simon & Schuster, LLC.
All rights reserved, including the right of reproduction in whole or in part in any form.
LITTLE SIMON is a registered trademark of Simon & Schuster, LLC,
and associated colophon is a trademark of Simon & Schuster, LLC.
For information about special discounts for bulk purchases,
please contact Simon & Schuster Special Sales at 1-866-506-1949
or business@simonandschuster.com.
The Simon & Schuster Speakers Bureau can bring authors to your live event.
For more information or to book an event,
contact the Simon & Schuster Speakers Bureau at 1-866-248-3049
or visit our website at www.simonspeakers.com.
Book design by Leslie Mechanic based on the series design by Steve Scott
Manufactured in the United States of America 0525 MTN
2 4 6 8 10 9 7 6 5 3 1
Library of Congress Control Number 2025935324
ISBN 9781665988810
ISBN 9781534410404 (*The Haunted House Next Door* ebook)
ISBN 9781534410435 (*Ghost Don't Ride Bikes, Do They?* ebook)
ISBN 9781534418035 (*Surf's Up, Creepy Stuff!* ebook)
These titles were previously published individually by Little Simon.

CONTENTS

 Haunted House Next Door   5

 Ghosts Don't Ride Bikes, Do They?   130

 Surf's Up, Creepy Stuff!   256

DESMOND COLE
GHOST PATROL

THE HAUNTED HOUSE NEXT DOOR

CONTENTS

Chapter One: Welcome to Kersville — 7

Chapter Two: Normal-Boring Happy — 23

Chapter Three: Whatevs — 33

Chapter Four: A Hand in the Night — 47

Chapter Five: The Silverware Man — 57

Chapter Six: Grape Secrets — 73

Chapter Seven: The Flying Table — 85

Chapter Eight: A Most Haunted Lasagna — 95

Chapter Nine: Ghost Gunk — 111

Chapter Ten: Meet the Ghost Patrol — 125

CHAPTER ONE

WELCOME TO KERSVILLE

When you move to a new town, grown-ups always give you a lot of advice. They say you should explore your new neighborhood right away. They say you should make new friends as soon as possible.

They never tell you what to do if your house is haunted.

Good thing I live next door to the coolest, bravest kid in the world. That's him, but he's busy right now. You would be too if a ghost was trying to slime you!

His name is Desmond Cole.

DESMOND COLE

Me? I'm Andres Miedoso, and I'm definitely *not* the coolest and bravest kid in the world.

Do you see me?

ANDRES MIEDOSO

Look behind our brand-new sofa. That's my foot, and it's quivering with fear. Do you want to know why? Well, look up.

Yep. That's a ghost. He's seconds away from sliming our brand-new sofa . . . and me!

But wait.

There's another thing grown-ups tell kids. They always say you have to start at the beginning.

It all began yesterday, when my parents and I moved to Kersville. We pulled in front of our new place, and the movers were already there with trucks blocking the driveway.

"Isn't it a beautiful house?" Mom asked, turning around in her seat.

"It's okay," I mumbled.

"I know you're nervous about moving, *mi hijo*," she said. "But there's nothing to worry about."

Mom and Dad got out of the car, and I followed behind them slowly.

That was when I heard something coming from next door. The garage door opened, and two boys came out. They shook hands, and one boy walked away.

"There's a boy your age right next door," Mom said. "See how lucky you are, Andres! Go and make friends."

Mom made everything sound so easy.

"Go on," Dad said. "Have some fun."

"All right," I mumbled.

That was when the boy next door waved to me. "Can you come over?" he asked.

I nodded and walked over. With his garage door open, I could see that it looked more like an office inside. There was an old desk, two chairs, and a bookcase full of thick books.

On the desk there was a flashlight, a video camera, walkie-talkies, and some weird gadgets with numbers on them. I started to get a little nervous.

"Hey," the boy said, smiling. "I'm Desmond Cole."

"Um, I'm Andres Miedoso."

"This is a great neighborhood," Desmond said. "Well, except for —"

"What is that?" I asked, spotting some odd-looking glasses hanging on the wall.

"Those are night-vision goggles," he replied.

"*Night-vision goggles?*" I asked, but Desmond interrupted me.

"Andres, I have to warn you."

Warn me? Now I was getting nervous.

"It's my mom," he said. "She's making a welcome lasagna for your family."

"That sounds nice," I said.

Desmond leaned in close to me. "Don't eat it. Trust me. My mom is a pretty terrible cook." Then he laughed.

I tried to laugh too, but this kid and his strange garage-office were freaking me out. "Um, I'd better go now."

"Here," Desmond said, handing me a business card.

"Uh, um, thanks," I said, and slowly backed away. "S-see you around."

I ran home thinking about how much I never wanted to see him again. *Never.*

Of course, that was before I knew what it was like living in Kersville. Everybody needed a friend like Desmond Cole in this town.

CHAPTER TWO

NORMAL-BORING HAPPY

Mom and Dad were busy with the movers, so I decided to check out the new house. After meeting Desmond, I needed time to get my heartbeat back to its normal speed.

Even though there were boxes everywhere and the furniture wasn't

where it was supposed to be, the house was normal. Normal and boring.

A normal-boring front door and a normal-boring den.

A normal-boring kitchen and a normal-boring dining room.

There were four normal-boring bedrooms and two normal-boring bathrooms.

The front yard and the garage were . . . well, you get it.

The thing is, I like normal-boring. I understand normal-boring.

Maybe that's because I'm normal-boring too.

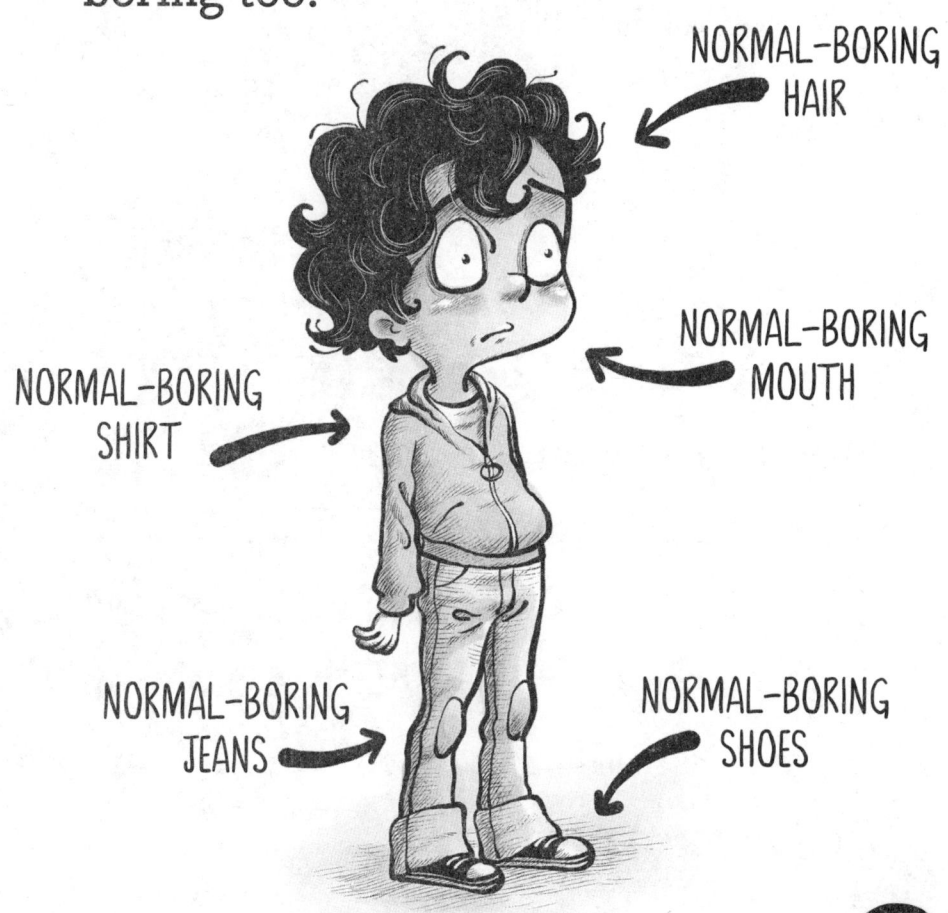

The only thing that wasn't normal-boring about this house was the basement. The stairs creaked as I walked down. It was almost completely dark except for a little light that came in from a small window. There were shadows everywhere.

There were also pipes that made clanging noises, and I jumped every single time they clanked.

I ran back upstairs. Sure, most basements were creepy, but I didn't want to take any chances. I like the normal-boring parts of the house, thank you very much.

Mom was in the den. "Did you get along with the boy next door?"

she asked me. "Wouldn't it be great if you found a best friend on your first day here?"

"Mom, nobody becomes best friends in two minutes! That would be a world record!"

"I just want you to be happy here in Kersville," she said.

"I'm happy," I told her. "And yeah, Desmond is pretty cool."

She smiled. "Good."

I didn't want Mom to worry about me, but the truth is, I wasn't sure Desmond Cole would make a good best friend. Something about him seemed . . . strange.

I went upstairs to my new room and started unpacking. I wanted my room to look the way it did in my last house and the house before that. Normal-boring.

Maybe Kersville would be as normal-boring as my room. But something told me I wouldn't be so lucky.

CHAPTER THREE

WHATEVS

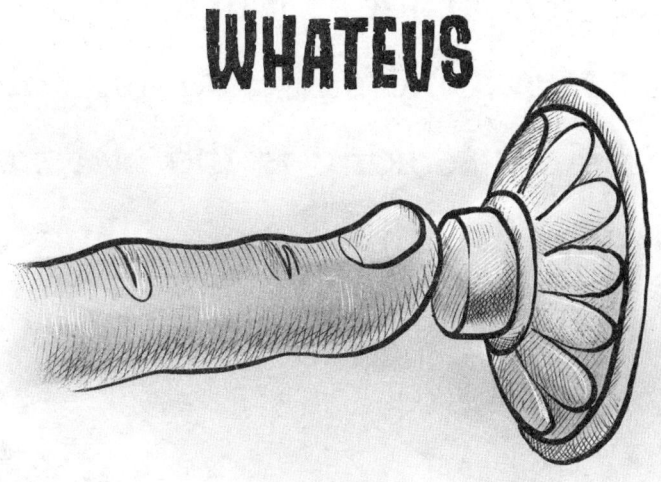

DING-DONG! That evening, the doorbell rang. It was Desmond and his parents, and sure enough, his mom was carrying a casserole dish. I was super-hungry, but that was probably the lasagna Desmond told me about—no, *warned me about.*

Everyone introduced themselves and came inside. "I made this for you," Mrs. Cole said, handing Mom the dish. "Cooking is the last thing you need to think about when you move into a new house."

Mom thanked Mrs. Cole. Then she said, "Andres, why don't you show Desmond your new room?"

"Okay," I said. I knew she just wanted to talk to the grown-ups without us kids around. And that was fine with me.

On the way upstairs, Desmond stopped short. "What's wrong?" I asked, but he didn't say anything.

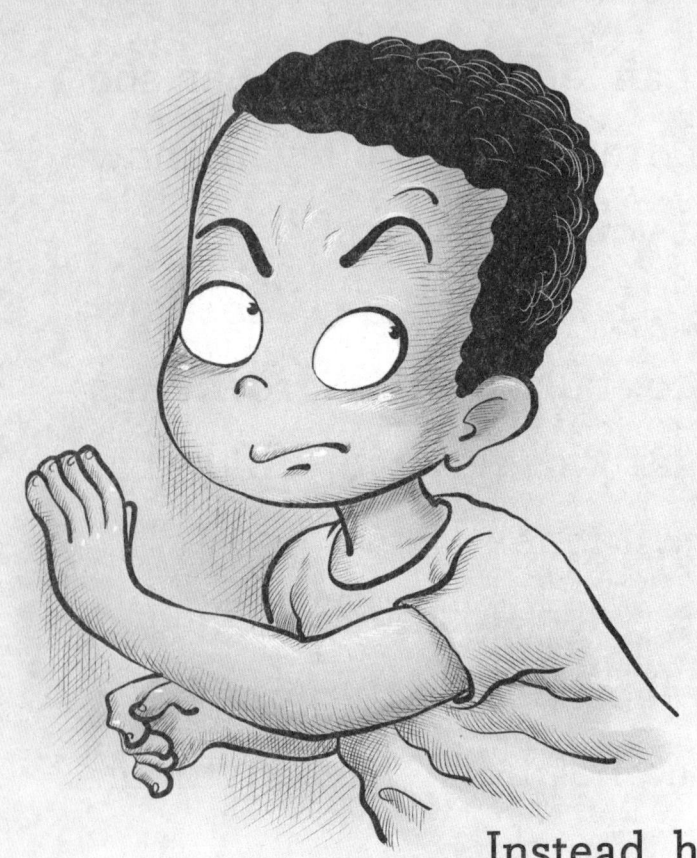

Instead, he tapped the wall and put his ear to it. My panicky feeling came back. "Wh-what are y-you . . . ?"

"Shhh." He listened to the wall.

Then he blew out puffs of air all around. After that he licked his finger and held it up into the air. None of this made any sense to me.

"What are you doing?" I finally asked.

He shrugged. "Oh, sorry. That's just something I do."

"Okay," I said. "Whatevs."

We walked into my room. Covering one wall was a gigantic poster of the entire solar system. The poster was so huge it made my room feel like it was in outer space.

"Oh wow!" Desmond exclaimed. "That's the coolest thing I ever saw."

"Yeah, my dad got it for me," I told

Desmond. "It's the first thing I put on my wall whenever we move."

That poster made every place feel like home.

"You're a space fan, huh?" asked Desmond.

"What was your clue, Sherlock?" I asked, and we both laughed.

Desmond looked around the rest of my room. "So what brings you to Kersville?"

"My parents are scientists working on a top secret project for the government," I said. "Oops. I probably shouldn't have told you that."

"Wait, seriously?" Desmond asked.

I nodded, because really, it was true.

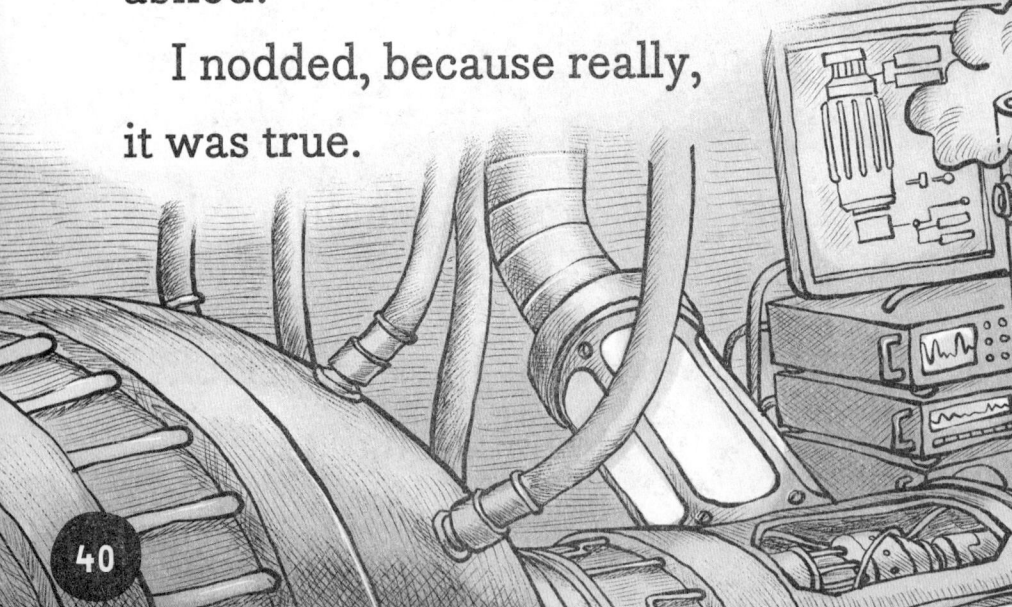

"Your secret's safe with me," he said. "It must be cool to have top secret parents."

"Yeah, but we have to move a lot," I said. "Normally, we don't even stay in the same town for a year."

"Kersville isn't normal," Desmond said. "When people move here, they stay."

"I hope so," I said.

That was when Mom called from downstairs. "Hey, Andres, Desmond's parents are leaving now."

Before we left the room, Desmond tapped walls and blew out his breath.

But this time,
he jumped back,
as if he saw
something.

"Huh?" was all he said. Then Desmond licked his finger and held it into the air again. "Uh, you still have my card I gave you, right?"

My heart beat hard. "Um, why?"

"Call me if you need me, okay?"

"N-need you?" I asked.

Desmond smiled. "Yeah, like if you want me to show you around. We have a new comic book store and

a bike park. With a bike like yours, I know you ride."

Back downstairs, Desmond left with his parents. But I couldn't stop thinking about those weird things he had done or what made him jump.

Most of all, I couldn't stop wondering why he thought I would need him.

CHAPTER FOUR

A Hand in the Night

That night, we ordered pizza for dinner and had a picnic on the living-room floor. Most of our plates were still in boxes, and we were too tired to find them. "We'll save Mrs. Cole's lasagna for tomorrow," Mom said, and I secretly smiled.

After dinner, I went to bed earlier than usual. As I walked into my bedroom, I tapped the wall like Desmond had done. Nothing happened.

I laughed to myself. *What did I think was going to happen?*

Then I heard it.

TAP TAP TAP.

I covered my mouth with my hand and stood still, listening hard. I waited, as stiff as a statue, but the wall was quiet.

Finally, I let myself breathe again. *It's just my imagination,* I thought.

Not only that, I was dog tired. I climbed into bed and read a few pages of my favorite book, but even that couldn't keep me awake. I fell fast asleep with the lights on.

I was freezing when I woke up. My eyes popped open, and I looked around the pitch-black room. I wasn't even sure where I was at first. Then I remembered: I was in my new room. *But why is it colder than outer space?* I thought. *And who turned off the lights?*

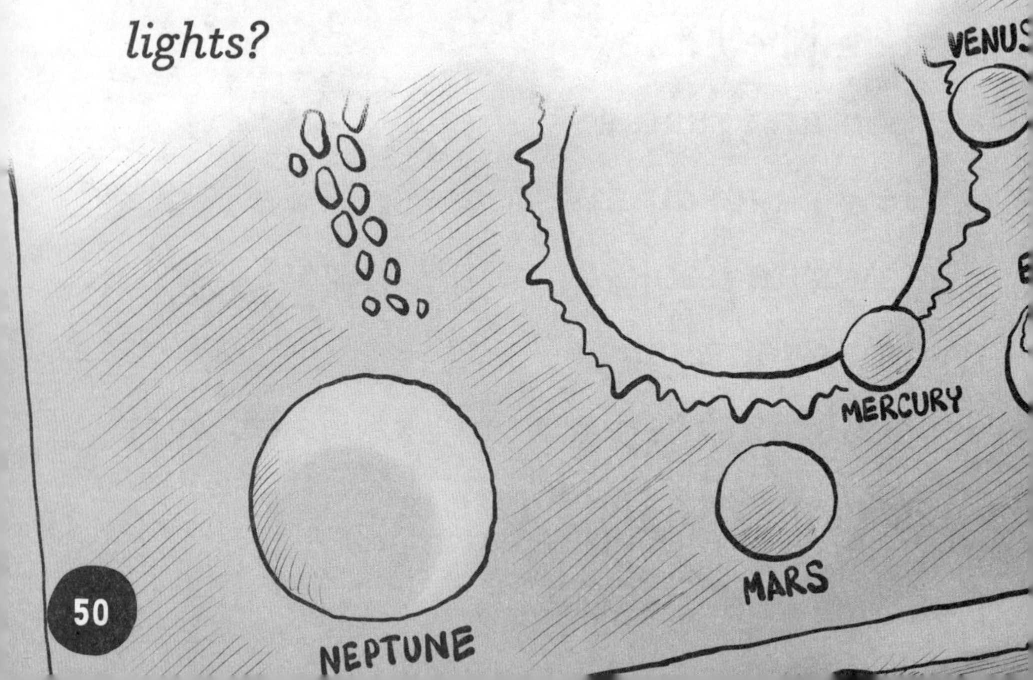

I blew out a huge breath of air, just like Desmond had done. In the darkness, my breath became a fuzzy white cloud that floated around my room. *That's not right.*

So I did Desmond's next trick. I put my finger in my mouth and then held it up. Bright blue sparks shot out from my finger, and shock waves ran through my body.

The lights started flashing *by themselves*, and when I saw my reflection in the mirror, I looked like a bolt of lightning had hit my head.

I sat there in bed, frozen with fear. That's when I heard a creaking sound coming from the walls. I dove under the covers—they were my only protection. Then something touched me. *It was a hand!*

"Andres?" Mom's voice was soft.

I peeked from under the blanket, and my heart skipped a beat. Mom was standing over my bed. She sat down.

"You were having a bad dream." She picked the book off my bed and put it on the night table. Then she leaned over and kissed me on the forehead. "Go back to sleep, and I'll turn off the light."

"Okay," I said. "Good night, Mom."

"Good night, *mi hijo*."

Sure, it's embarrassing that Mom had to tuck me in like a little kid. But after those crazy things happened, I did *not* mind at all.

CHAPTER FIVE

THE SILVERWARE MAN

The very next day was all about unpacking boxes.

And lifting heavy things.

And moving those heavy things to just the right spot.

While Mom unpacked clothes and books, Dad and I moved furniture.

Yeah, I was sweaty and tired, but I love putting things where they belong.

Dad and I saved the den for last. We had to lift giant chairs and a brand-new sofa, then set up the TV

and sound system. When everything was in place, we collapsed on the sofa, breathing hard.

Dad declared, "It's official. This house is our home. And to celebrate, we need my famous lemonade."

Dad thinks his lemonade is the greatest thing in the world. And actually, it is.

He went into the kitchen. As I followed him, there was a loud crash behind me. I spun around, thinking something fell over, but what I saw was...

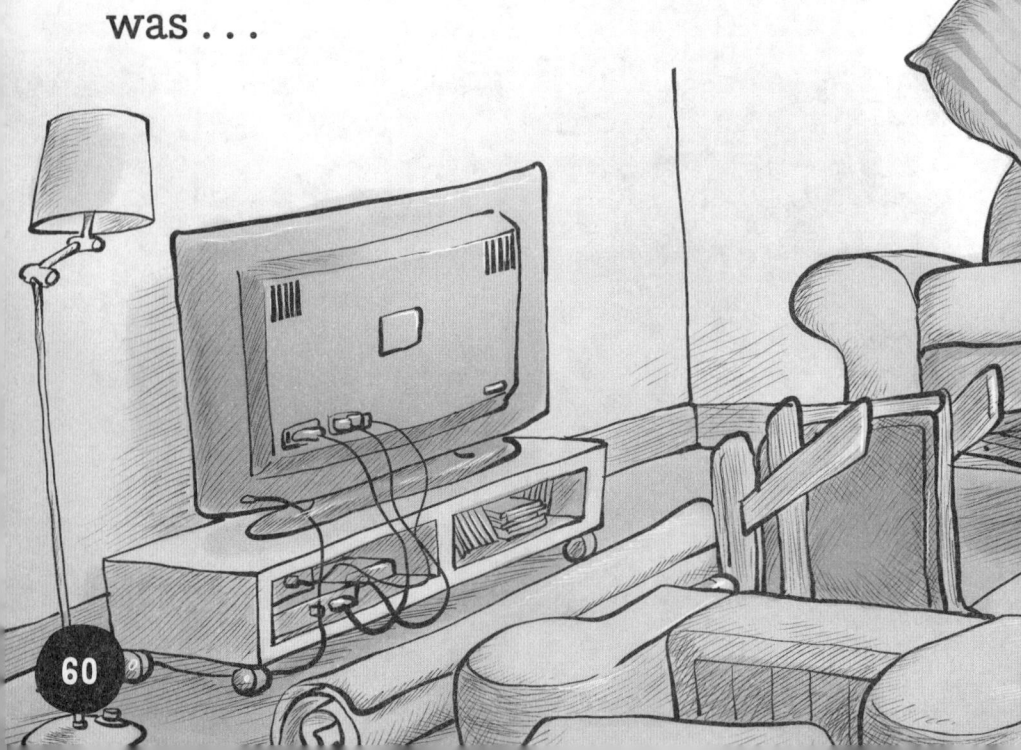

How can I explain it?

In the two seconds my back was turned, the entire room had changed! All the furniture was rearranged, and the sofa was now floating, like, way up in the air.

"Dad! Dad!" I raced into the kitchen. "You have to see this!"

I grabbed him by the arm and pulled him into the den. But the furniture was back exactly the way Dad and I had arranged it. You never would have known anything had been out of place.

"What do I have to see?" Dad asked, sounding confused.

I just stood there with my mouth open. "Um, nothing," I mumbled. "I thought—forget it."

I couldn't tell Dad what had just happened. He would think I was losing my mind. Maybe I *was* losing my mind.

Dad shrugged. "Well, okay. Let's go get that lemonade. I'll bet you're thirsty!" He laughed and put his arm around me as we walked.

Mom had already unpacked the kitchen. It was normal-boring and spotless, just the way I like it. I tried to relax. "Everything is going to be okay," I told myself.

Dad was grabbing a pitcher from the cabinet when Mom called from upstairs. "Honey, can you give me a hand?"

"Okay," Dad said. "Lemonade when I get back, Andres. I promise."

I nodded and then closed my eyes. Maybe the den was just a weird daydream?

Then I opened my eyes and gasped. Every drawer and cabinet

in the kitchen was open. Cups and plates were piled on top of the table and counter, and our silverware was scattered on the floor.

I went to scream, but before the sound came out, the forks, knives,

and spoons all slowly moved around in a circle. It looked like a tornado. As they spun around, they started to form into something that looked . . . human. It was a . . .

...GIANT SILVERWARE MAN!

That was all I needed to see, so I took off and ran out the front door. I didn't even look where I was going. And as soon as I made it outside,

I slammed into something—no, *someone*.

I ran smack into Desmond Cole.

CHAPTER SIX

GRAPE SECRETS

"OOF!"

That was what Desmond said as I knocked the wind out of him. He sank into a heap on the ground.

"Sorry, sorry, sorry," I said, helping him back up. "I didn't mean— um, I didn't see you standing . . ."

"It's okay," Desmond said. "But seriously, dude, what's your rush?"

My mind was still racing from what I had just seen in the kitchen. No way was I going to tell Desmond what had just happened. No way was I going to tell *anyone*.

So I played it cool and searched for my calm voice. "I just, um, have to go to the store. You know, for my parents."

"Cool," Desmond said. "I'll walk you there."

"Okay."

On the way, I tried to hide how scared I was, but my legs were still a little wobbly. And my hands were still a little shaky.

I don't think Desmond noticed, though. He was too busy talking to people we passed on the street. It seemed like everybody in Kersville knew Desmond. One boy told him,

"Thanks for everything the other day."

"Glad I could help," Desmond said.

Then we passed a girl who said, "Hey, thanks, Desmond."

"Call if you need me again," he replied.

Finally, I had to ask, "What did you do for those kids?"

But Desmond changed the subject. "Did you eat my mom's lasagna yet?"

"Um, no, not yet," I told him. "We always have pizza the first night in a new home. It's a tradition with us."

When we reached the store, Desmond asked, "What did your parents want you to buy?"

I had no idea what to tell him. "I'm supposed to get, um, grapes."

Okay, I know that wasn't the best answer, but I could barely concentrate on what I was saying. My head was spinning with questions. *How did Desmond help all those kids? And*

why didn't he want to tell me? And what in the world was happening back at my not-so-normal, not-at-all-boring house?!

Then, almost like he was reading my mind, Desmond asked, "Have you discovered any secrets at the new house?"

Whoa, that was all I needed to hear. I was off running again, this time *away* from Desmond. Sure, I was making a complete fool out of myself, but I just wanted to leave him and his mind-reading questions behind.

I found the way back to my house, sprinted inside, and closed the door behind me.

That's when it hit me: I wasn't safe here, either.

CHAPTER SEVEN

THE FLYING TABLE

Inside the house, everything looked normal. The furniture was where it was supposed to be, and nothing appeared to be moving on its own.

Mom and Dad were hanging up pictures and asked for my help. They know I love hammering nails!

After the last picture was hung, Mom said it was time for lunch and asked me to set the table.

I walked to the kitchen as slowly as possible and peeked inside. Luckily, there weren't any scary silverware people.

As I put out plates, Dad poured his world-famous lemonade, and Mom heated up Mrs. Cole's lasagna.

Mom put the dish on the table, and that lasagna looked and smelled delicious. I wanted to dig right in, but I could hear Desmond in my head, warning me to stay away from it.

So I let Mom and Dad get some first, and I watched as they ate. They both took little bites at first, and then they started shoveling the food into their mouths, like it was the best thing they had ever eaten.

First I heard: "Ooh" and "Yum" and "Ahhh."

Then I heard: "Uh-oh" and "Oh no" and "Ugh."

That was when Mom and Dad sprang from the table. Their stomachs were making awful gurgling noises like tiny angry monsters. Then they ran out of the kitchen like two bolts of lightning and headed in opposite directions toward the two bathrooms.

Right away, both bathroom fans went on. But that didn't stop me from hearing way too many noises coming from inside.

"Ew, gross," I said to myself.

I pushed my plate away and got up from the table. On the counter, there was a bowl of—what else—grapes. I grabbed a handful and took a bite of one.

That was when I felt a cold gust of wind behind me. *What could it be now?*

I hoped it was just my mind playing tricks on me again. But it wasn't. What I saw was all too real.

The entire kitchen table—dish of lasagna and all—was floating high into the air.

I dropped my grapes on the floor and screamed.

CHAPTER EIGHT

A Most Haunted Lasagna

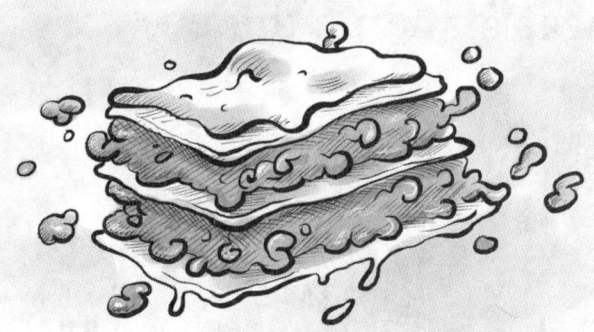

As the table rose higher and higher, so did my scream.

I tried to move, but it took me a few long seconds to make my legs work.

Then, just like before, I ran from the room.

And, just like before, I opened the front door.

And, yes, just like before, Desmond Cole was standing there.

This time I didn't slam into him, which was a good thing because he was carrying some weird gadget. It made a whirring noise, and it had blinking lights.

I was shaking too much to talk, but Desmond had a huge smile on his face. "I knew it!" he exclaimed. "You brought a ghost with you, didn't you?"

He was so excited, he didn't even wait for me to invite him inside. He just pushed past me and ran into my house.

"What are you talking about?" I asked. "Me? Bring a ghost? *A ghost?*"

Desmond ran into the den and looked around. "Well, if you didn't bring it, then you're one lucky guy."

"Lucky?!" I said. Okay, this kid was bonkers.

"Yeah!" Desmond smiled as he waved his machine around. "Don't you get it? You are living in a haunted house!"

My heart stopped. "A haunted what?"

"Stop asking so many questions," Desmond said, walking through the den, pointing his gadget at the walls and the sofa and the TV. "Don't tell me you've never heard of a haunted house."

"I've *heard* of them," I said. "But I don't want to *live* in one. Can you do something about it?"

"Of course!" Desmond said.

"You moved to the haunted house next door to the right kid."

Desmond's gadget was making louder and louder beeps as he moved closer to the kitchen. I followed behind him. *Far* behind him.

"Whoa," he exclaimed, stepping into the room. "Does your table always fly like that?"

I shook my head. "Not usually."

"Good," Desmond said. "Because that would be really weird. But also kind of cool!" He didn't look scared at all. In fact, he looked like this was the most fun he'd ever had.

Desmond jumped up and grabbed one of the legs of the table and pulled it back down to the floor. We were face-to-face with the lasagna.

To be honest, it still looked really delicious.

"You didn't actually eat that, right?" Desmond asked.

"Not me." I motioned to the bathrooms. "My parents did and . . ."

Desmond shook his head and gagged a little. "Say no more."

Then without warning, the lasagna lifted out of the dish and floated above the table. I ducked behind Desmond and whimpered, "A haunted lasagna? Now I've seen everything!"

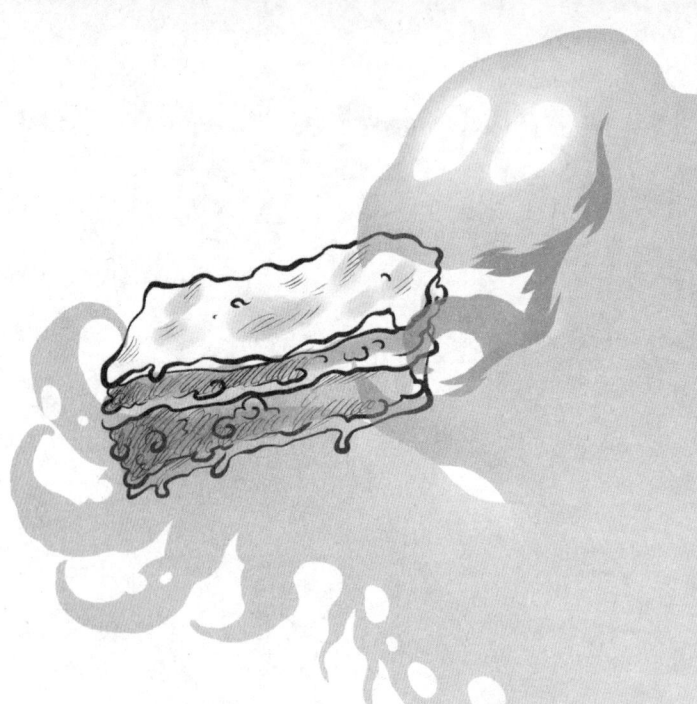

But I hadn't seen everything. Because when I looked again, the lasagna wasn't floating by itself. No. A ghost appeared out of thin air, and it was holding the lasagna in its ghostly hands. It sniffed the food with its ghostly nose and then gobbled the whole thing up with its ghostly mouth.

"This is not good," whispered Desmond. "This is not good at all."

Suddenly, the ghost turned green; puffed out its ghostly cheeks; and let out a loud, wet, disgusting burp.

It. Was. Gross.

If you've never smelled a ghost burp, consider yourself lucky!

"Ewww," I moaned.

The ghost puffed its ghostly cheeks again, but before it could burp again, Desmond yelled, "Run!"

And that was exactly what we did!

CHAPTER NINE
GHOST GUNK

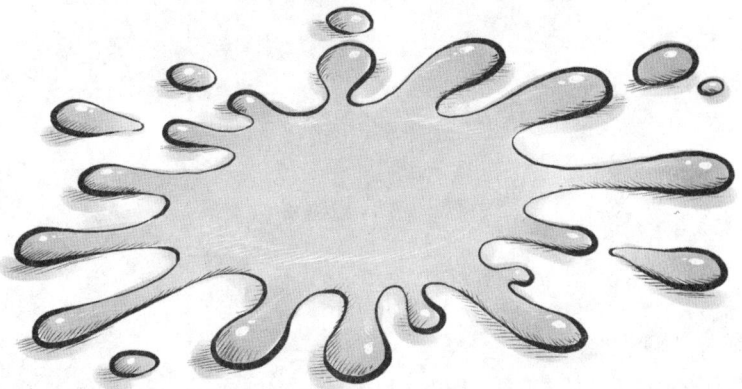

So here we are, where the story started. I wish I could say the ghost stayed in the kitchen. Or went back to wherever ghosts come from. But we weren't that lucky.

The ghost followed us into the den. And that's how I ended up here, hiding behind the brand-new sofa. Shivering and quivering.

Don't judge me, though. You would be hiding too if there was a large gross burping ghost floating over your head. The ghost looked like it was going to be really, really, really sick all over the brand-new sofa.

And me.

Good thing Desmond was there. That kid wasn't scared at all. He looked up at the ghost and said, "Hello, I'm Desmond Cole, Ghost Patrol. You are in a home that is owned by this human, Andres Miedoso."

The ghost let out another burp, and this one stank even worse than the last. I covered my nose with my hand, but I could still smell it. That was when the ghost turned its head to look at me. I started to shiver and quiver at top speed.

"You own this house?" the ghost asked me in an eerie, raspy voice.

A ghost was talking to me.

"Um," I began. "My, uh, parents own the house."

"Are your parents human?" the ghost asked as it moved closer to me.

"Yes, I think so." I looked over to Desmond, who nodded and gave me a *duh* look, as if to say, *Of course your parents are human.*

Then the ghost turned back to Desmond. "What did I eat? It looked good, but it makes me feel so bad."

"I'm sorry about that," Desmond said. "My mom made it, but it wasn't for you."

"Is that what human food always tastes like?" the ghost asked, and it burped again.

"No," Desmond said. "Only when my mom makes it."

As the ghost hovered above us, I could hear its stomach making the same kind of monster noises my parents' stomachs had made.

Desmond cleared his throat. "I know you are not feeling well," he told the ghost. "But I need you to leave this house. Do you have anywhere else to go?"

"No," said the ghost. It lowered its ghost eyes. "I move from one house to another all the time. I do not have a home."

Well, well, well, I couldn't believe it. I actually started to feel sorry for that ghost because I knew exactly how it felt to move all the time. Now the ghost didn't seem so scary. It just looked sad.

"Um, maybe you can stay here . . . in our basement?" I did not expect to hear those words come out of my mouth, but they did. "I mean, if you promise not to do any spooky stuff, like what you did with the silverware and the kitchen table. Do you think you can *not* do that?"

That was when the ghost smiled. "Yes! Yes! Thank you! Thank you!" It looked so happy. It raised its arms to give me hug and said, "I promise to always be on my best behav—"

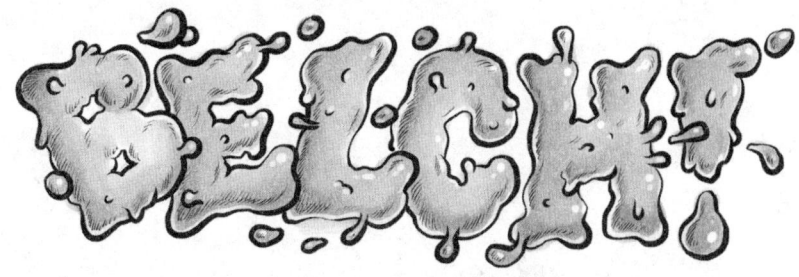

It was the loudest, ghostliest belch on the planet. It was followed by the ghastliest, grossliest gunk in the universe. And it landed all over our brand-new sofa.

And all over me.

CHAPTER TEN

MEET THE GHOST PATROL

Turns out, the ghost's name is Zax, and he's actually pretty cool . . . well, for a ghost. He tries to keep his promise and not scare me, and he never bothers my parents at all.

Actually, living with Zax is like having a little brother. He always floats through my walls uninvited, takes my stuff without asking, and reads my books before I'm finished with them. But I don't mind . . . most of the time.

Even if I did, I wouldn't say anything. Let me tell you, it's really hard to wash off ghost gunk. It's something I only want to do once!

As for Desmond, he's my best friend now. Even though

he couldn't stop me from being, um, slimed, he did solve my haunted house problem. Well, my house is still haunted, but now I know it's only because of Zax.

Life in Kersville is getting better and better. I have a ghost *and* a new best friend. Oh yeah, I have a new after-school job, too. I joined the Ghost Patrol. Desmond says it's easier with more than one person.

Right now, my biggest fear is that my parents will tell me it's time to move again. That would be the worst because I kind of really like it here.

Desmond gets calls all the time from kids who need his help—no, *our* help. That's what makes Kersville such an unusual place. You never know what's going to happen next. And believe it or not, I like that.

DESMOND COLE GHOST PATROL

GHOSTS DON'T RIDE BIKES, DO THEY?

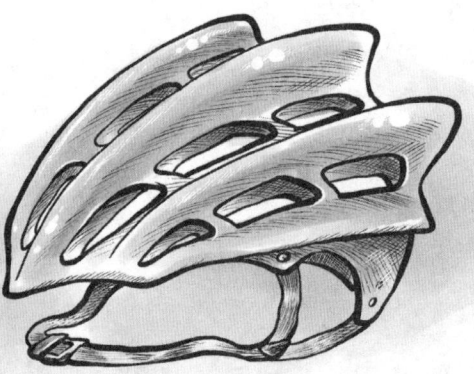

CONTENTS

Chapter One: Thrills and Spills   133

Chapter Two: Ghost Secrets   141

Chapter Three: The Kicker   151

Chapter Four: Cheddar Cheese Fish Fries   163

Chapter Five: Kersville Elementary School   175

Chapter Six: Game Over, Ghost!   187

Chapter Seven: Ghost Tricks   201

Chapter Eight: A New Case   225

Chapter Nine: Desmond's Daring Run   233

Chapter Ten: Hal the Bike Healer   251

CHAPTER ONE
THRILLS AND SPILLS

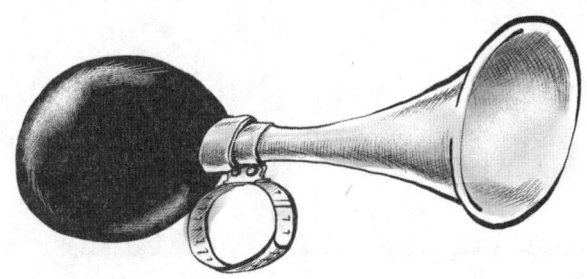

Let's talk about the thrills and spills of riding a bike. Is there anything more thrilling than racing down the street with the wind in your face? Even the spills are cool. Trying to do a trick and falling off your bike, or coming home with a brand-new hole in your jeans—it's the best! Thrills and spills. You can't have one without the other. And I wouldn't want it any other way.

The thing is, nobody ever talks about the *chills* of riding a bike. At least not until I moved to Kersville. This town is made of chills!

My bike is the coolest thing in the world. It's black with red rims. The handlebars have a compass on one side, a light in the middle, and a horn on the other side. Not a bell. A horn!

What I love about my bike is that it's not shiny and new. This bike has been through a lot of spills. There are scratches on the paint and dents to prove it. The seat even has a piece of black electrical tape from when I crashed trying to ride backward—bad idea.

The thing is, even though my bike isn't perfect, it's all mine. It's moved to every new house we've moved to, and it feels the same no matter where I live. It's basically been my best friend.

I have a real friend now. His name is Desmond Cole. He never cared about bikes before. Why?

Well, do you see that bike over there—the one with the compass, the light, and the horn? The one with the scratch on the frame and

the electrical tape on the seat? The one that's riding through the forest without anyone on it?

Yep, that's my bike.

Why is the bike riding by itself?

Well, that's a strange story.

CHAPTER TWO

GHOST SECRETS

Last week I introduced Desmond to my most prized possession in the whole world: my bike.

I opened the garage, and my bike was right there in its own spot. The sun streamed into the garage, and the light made my bike glow.

"What do you think?" I asked.

"A bike?" Desmond said flatly. "I guess it's cool."

"It's cooler than cool," I said. "Want to go riding?"

"I don't do bikes," Desmond said.

I was shocked. "Why not?"

"Because I like ghosts," he said.

What do ghosts have to do with bikes? I wondered.

Desmond must have been reading my mind. "Ghosts don't ride bikes," he said, like it was something everybody in the world already knew.

That was when Zax floated through the wall. He's a ghost, so it's not as weird as it sounds. "Andres, I need a ratchet from the toolbox."

"Wait, Zax," I said. "Let me ask you a question. Is it true that ghosts don't ride bikes?"

"Of course ghosts don't ride bikes," Zax said. Then he let out a hearty laugh that was almost as loud as his burps.

"Why not?" I asked.

"Birds don't ride bikes, do they?" Zax replied.

"Um, no," I said.

Desmond nodded. "See what I mean, Andres?"

To be honest, I was still confused.

Zax looked up from the toolbox. "Why would ghosts ride bikes when we can float everywhere?"

"Um, because riding a bike is awesome!" I said. "Speaking of awesome, I hear the Kersville Bike Park has a crazy racetrack!"

Desmond shrugged. "There won't be any ghosts there, so count me out. Have fun, and I'll see you later."

He waved good-bye and went next door into his own garage. That's where he had his Ghost Patrol office. I guess Desmond liked ghosts as much as I liked my bike.

"Found it!" Zax exclaimed, holding up the ratchet. He closed the toolbox and floated straight toward the wall. He almost made it through, but then I heard a loud **CLANG**. The ratchet dropped and smacked against the floor.

"Oh yeah," Zax said. He floated into the garage. "I keep forgetting not everything can go through walls. Can you carry this for me?"

"Okay." I kicked off my gear and took the tool. "What are you doing with this, anyway?"

Zax smiled. "It's a secret."

A secret? Something told me I wasn't going to like ghost secrets. But I put it out of my mind. I had better things to do. I had a bike park to check out!

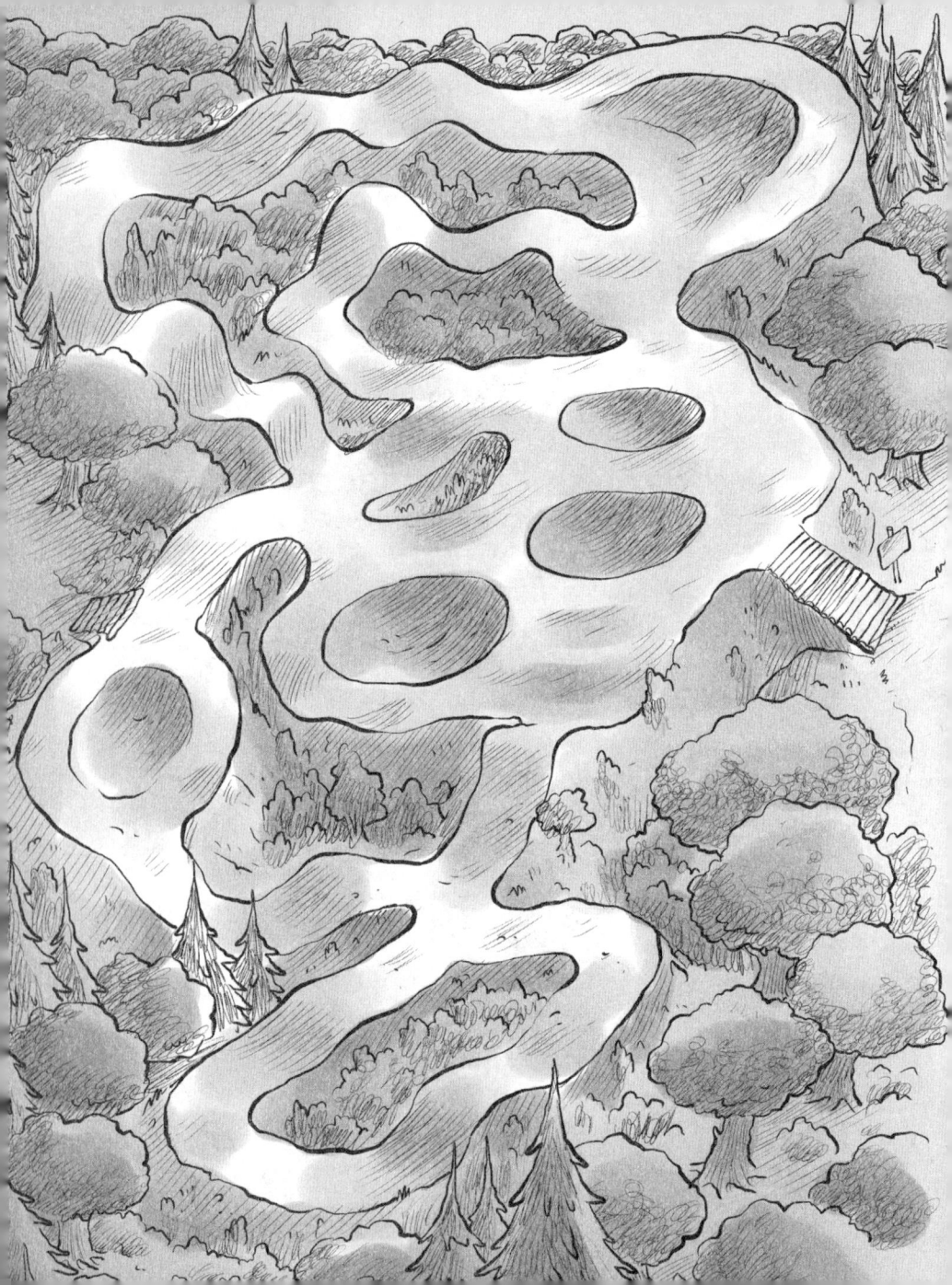

CHAPTER THREE

THE KICKER

KERSVILLE BIKE PARK

When my parents decided to move to Kersville, they told me the town had a bike park close to our new house. That made moving here a lot easier.

The park turned out to be awesome. It had a huge dirt racetrack with way too many jumps to count.

I was prepared, though. I was wearing my helmet, kneepads, elbow pads, *and* bike gloves.

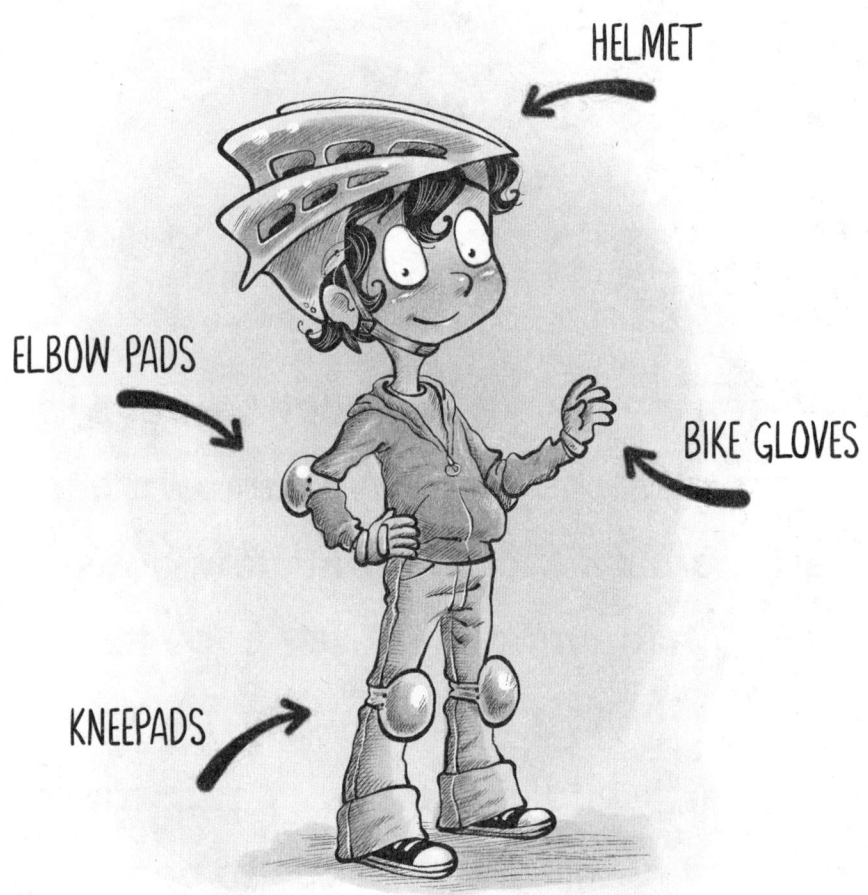

I rode over to the start of the track and waited behind a group of other kids.

"Hey, you're new here," said the boy in front of me. He pointed to the end of the track. "Whatever you do, don't ride that last jump. It's called the Kicker. Nobody ever lands it."

"Nobody?" I gulped.

"Watch and learn," he said.

A rider sped around the last turn toward the Kicker. Suddenly, her front tire lifted up into a wheelie and the girl fell off her bike. But her bike kept going! It flew up the ramp and crash-landed on the other side.

The girl got up and brushed herself off.

"The Kicker strikes again," the boy told me.

While I waited my turn, one rider after another wiped out on the Kicker. It was weird. I mean, everybody fell! Sometimes they fell to the left. Sometimes they fell to the right. One kid ended up doing a backflip into the dirt. Each time, the bike still took the jump and crashed.

I was nervous. I was a good bike rider, but I had never tried anything like the Kicker before.

Finally, it was my turn. I pedaled down the first hill fast. The track

felt good as I whipped around the first turn. I hit the first jump, held on tight, and launched into the air. It was amazing!

I landed jump after jump, and pretty soon the other kids started cheering. *For me!*

Until I came to the Kicker. At first, everything was normal. Then I felt a wave of electricity sizzle through my body. My bike started to wobble. I gripped my handlebars as the bike jerked from side to side.

Next, my pedals began to speed up

and slow down. It felt like the gears were shifting on their own!

Still, I kept my bike under control and zoomed up the Kicker. I couldn't believe it. I was going to ace the track. All I had to do was land the jump.

I flew into the air, and, man, it was exciting! I was going to do it. I was going to—

SCREECH!

My bike froze in midair. I mean, it just stopped.

Unfortunately I kept on going, right over my handlebars into a mud puddle.

My bike crashed down a second later.

I had no idea what was going on, but I knew one thing for sure. The Kicker lived up to its name.

CHAPTER FOUR

CHEDDAR CHEESE FISH FRIES

Desmond came by my house that night, and he looked really scared.

"Please help me, Andres," he said. "There is a cooking experiment at my house tonight."

"What's a cooking experiment?" I asked.

Desmond shivered. "That's when my parents use all of our leftovers to make a new meal. They are making cheddar cheese fish fries with a marshmallow dipping sauce."

My family was just having homemade chicken nuggets, corn on the cob, and salad for dinner. All of a sudden it totally sounded like the best dinner in the world.

I could see that Desmond was in trouble. I invited him inside, and we walked to the kitchen. "Mom, can Desmond eat with us tonight?"

She was washing her hands in the sink. "Okay, as long as you kids set the table."

Desmond sniffed the air and smiled. "That's a small price to pay for saving my stomach . . . and my life!"

Mom and I laughed.

As we grabbed the plates, Dad came into the kitchen from the basement.

"Is something wrong with the water heater?" Mom asked him. "The water isn't getting hot."

"Oh yeah," I said. "I had the same problem when I took my shower."

Let me tell you, cold showers aren't fun.

Dad nodded. "Yeah, it's acting up. I can fix it, but some of my tools are missing. They must be in one of the boxes we haven't unpacked."

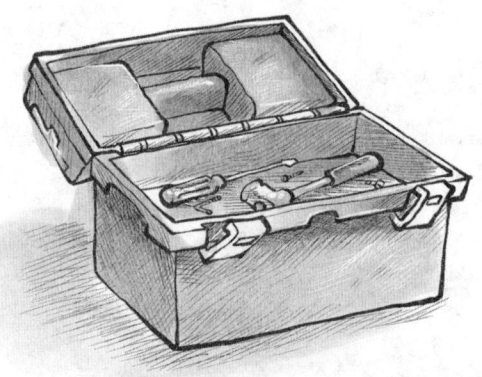

Desmond and I looked at each other. We didn't say a word, but I knew we were both thinking the same thing: *Zax*.

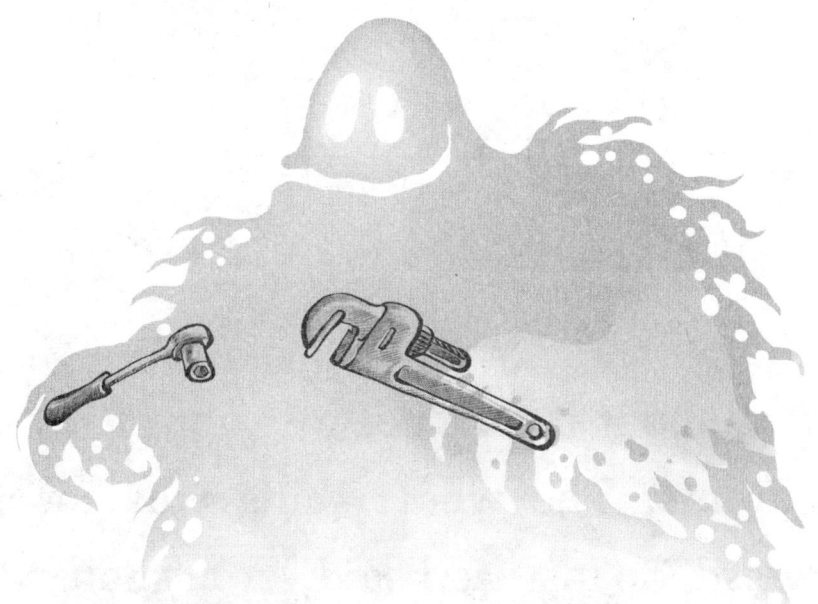

Desmond changed the subject. "How was the bike park?"

"Good," I said, and I wanted to tell

him about it, but not in front of my parents. The whole thing was too weird. So instead I said, "You should come next time. It's *scary* fun, if you catch my drift."

Desmond's eyes lit up. "For real?"

I nodded, and we finished setting the table. Then I grabbed Desmond, and we went into the garage. I filled him in on the strange way my bike had acted at the track.

He inspected my bike closely. "Was it only *your* bike that went wild?"

"Nope," I told him. "Everyone's bike did."

Desmond's eyes sparked with excitement. "Let's check it out tomorrow," he said. "But first, let's eat. I'm starving!"

CHAPTER FIVE

KERSVILLE ELEMENTARY SCHOOL

The next day, I rode my bike to Kersville Elementary. Hmm, how do I describe this school?

For starters, a long, long time ago, it was a mansion where the founder of the town lived. Then it was a hospital. Finally, it became a school.

But it still didn't *feel* like a school. Some of the classrooms used to be bedrooms, and the cafeteria used to be the ballroom in the mansion.

It had round tables and creaky old chairs. Plus, it had huge chandeliers hanging from the ceiling. Who puts fancy crystal lights in a school?

The gym used to be the mansion's barn. You could still smell the horse stalls, which meant the gym smelled *pee-yew* gross.

The first time I saw the school, I was too scared to get out of the car. My parents had to practically carry me inside!

I don't think it's *totally scary* anymore, just a little creepy. There had to be ghosts in that building. But this story is about bikes . . . kind of.

Desmond was waiting for me at the bike rack. "Were any of these bikes at the park yesterday?"

Most of the bikes weren't the kind you'd ride at the track. Some had curved handlebars. Some had tassels and baskets. A few even had training wheels.

Finally, I noticed two from the track. One belonged to the girl who I saw wipe out. The other belonged to the boy who'd warned me about the Kicker.

"Those two bikes were at the park," I told Desmond.

Desmond pulled a weird camera from his backpack. I had never seen a camera like this one. It looked like a video-game controller. I watched as Desmond popped up the flash and took a picture of the two bikes. But the flash created a shadow on the bikes instead of making everything bright.

Desmond looked at the screen and whistled. "Totally ghostly."

He turned the camera around so I could see the screen. In the picture, the two bikes were covered in glowing dust.

"Does my bike look like that too?" I asked.

"Probably," Desmond said. "But you live with a ghost. Everything in your house looks like this in the right light."

He put the camera away, and we walked toward the school. "I'm sure about one thing," Desmond said. "Something is definitely haunting the racetrack."

CHAPTER SIX

GAME OVER, GHOST!

After school, Desmond and I went to the bike park. The Ghost Patrol needed to figure out what was going on at the track.

The girl and the boy were riding and practicing tricks. They weren't going near the Kicker.

I whispered to Desmond, "I hope they ride the track so you can see how haunted it is."

"The track might not be haunted," Desmond said. "Their *bikes* might be haunted. That's why we have to watch them, to see if the bikes do

strange things on their own." He nodded at the girl. "Like that!"

I looked over and saw the girl's bike hop into the air a few times. Both tires came off the ground at the same time. "She's doing a bunny hop," I told Desmond. "It's a bike trick."

"Hey! What about that?" Desmond asked. The boy was balancing on his front tire. The back tire was up in the air.

"That's called a stoppie," I said.

"It's another trick. Wow, you really don't ride bikes, do you?"

Desmond shrugged. "I do not."

"Well, I ride bikes, and those bikes aren't haunted," I said.

After an hour of watching the boy and girl, Desmond couldn't take it anymore. He yelled, "Hey, how come you two aren't riding the Kicker today?"

"Ask your friend," the boy replied, pointing to me. "He fell so hard yesterday that no one else wants to ride it."

My face flushed hot. It was not cool being the kid *everybody* saw wipe out.

So in a flash, I hopped on my bike and put on

my helmet. There was only one way to prove the Kicker was haunted. I needed to ride the track again. But I had a plan this time.

I went to the top of the track and pedaled down the hill as fast as I could. I picked up speed with each turn and each jump.

"Go, Andres!" Desmond screamed. Everyone at the bike park clapped and cheered too.

Then, right before I reached the Kicker, I put my plan into action. I jumped off my bike.

As I crash-landed in the mud, all those cheers stopped.

My bike, on the other hand, kept going.

It jumped the Kicker, flew into a front flip, then landed perfectly and skidded to a stop. It was the craziest, coolest, creepiest thing ever! If I hadn't seen it with my own eyes, I wouldn't have believed it.

Thankfully, Desmond was right there. He knew what to do.

Desmond snapped a picture of my bike with his special camera. "Game over, ghost!" he announced. He ran over and showed me the screen.

What I saw made my heart do a front flip in my chest.

There was a ghost sitting on my bike, smiling from one ghostly ear to the other. And why wouldn't he be happy?

That ghost just landed the Kicker.

CHAPTER SEVEN

GHOST TRICKS

Slowly, the ghost appeared in real life. Everyone gasped. I gasped too, because that's what normal people do when they see a ghost.

"Did you see that trick?" the ghost asked excitedly and floated over to us. "It was awesome!"

I stood up from the mud. "Yeah, but you can't kick kids off bikes like that."

"It's not cool," added Desmond. "Not cool at all."

The ghost looked from Desmond to me to the other kids, who stood with their eyes wide open. Then he stopped smiling.

"Oh, I am so sorry," the ghost said. "I didn't mean to bother anyone. I just love this track. I've been flying around here for a long time, but I could never jump the Kicker. I'm a ghost, so I just pass right through the ramp every time."

I remembered Zax trying to pass through the wall with the ratchet. "You needed a real bike to jump the ramp."

The ghost nodded. "I only wanted to borrow one for a second."

"Maybe you could have asked first," I suggested.

"Yeah, I tried that once and scared a kid pretty bad," admitted the ghost. "But thanks to you, I finally landed the jump!"

"And you nailed it!" I cheered and high-fived the ghost.

"I know, right?" The ghost beamed.

Desmond was really excited. I could tell because he always asked questions when he was excited.  "How did you hold on to a moving bike? If you go up, do you have to come back down? Is riding a bike as a ghost easier than riding a bike as a not-ghost?"

"Those are ghost secrets, my friend," the ghost replied.

Now I'm positive that I don't like ghost secrets.

The ghost grabbed my bike and floated it back to me. "Here. Thank

you for helping my dream come true."

I took the handlebars and nodded to the ghost. "Hey, do you have a name?"

"You can call me Kicker," he said. Then Kicker faded away.

Desmond patted me on the back. "Congratulations, Andres. You just solved your first case!"

Now *I* was the one smiling. I have to admit, it felt great.

Back in my garage, Desmond studied my bike. I was wiping mud off my arms with a towel because there was no way I was going to take another cold shower. I'd rather be muddy *and* stinky.

Zax floated in looking for the toolbox again. He grabbed a wrench.

"Are you ever going to tell me what you're up to, Zax?" I asked.

"It's a surprise," he said. Then he floated back inside through the open door.

Desmond and I glanced at each other. We knew what we had to do.

We followed Zax and pressed up against the wall like spies. He went down to the basement and floated to the water heater. Desmond and I hid behind him on the dark stairs and watched.

Zax used the wrench to unscrew something.

Suddenly, I felt the icy chill of the truth. Zax definitely broke the water heater!

Before I could do anything, Zax said, "You guys can come out now. You're not very good at hiding."

Desmond and I stood up slowly.

"Did you break our water heater?" I asked. "I have been taking cold showers, you know!"

Zax put down the wrench. "I didn't break the water heater. I just fixed it."

"Fixed it?" I said. Then I turned to Desmond and asked, "Do ghosts fix stuff?"

Desmond shrugged like he had no idea.

Zax nodded. "Ghosts love to fix stuff. People hear clanging sounds and think we're haunting places, but that's just us fixing things. I love when everything runs smoothly."

"Wow," said Desmond. "I did not know that."

I couldn't believe it. Something Desmond Cole didn't know about ghosts? Now I'd heard it all.

"I need to go write this down in my ghost notebook," said Desmond as he took off up the stairs. "Thanks, Zax! And, Andres, please go take a shower. I didn't want to say anything, but you kinda smell."

"Oh yeah, ghosts can smell, too," admitted Zax as he held his nose. "Can you please go take a *long* shower?"

I laughed because he didn't have to tell me twice.

CHAPTER EIGHT

The next day after school, Desmond and I were still talking about Zax.

"Ghosts still surprise me," said Desmond. "They're always up to something new."

That was when a few of the kids from the bike park ran up to me. It was the first time I had seen them without their bikes.

"Andres!" exclaimed one of the girls. "You have to help us!"

"Yeah," another kid said. "Our bikes have been stolen. We think that ghost did it."

Desmond stepped in. "Hold on, everybody. Ghosts don't steal. At least, I don't think they steal."

I wasn't so sure. "This could be another ghost secret," I whispered to Desmond. "What if Kicker really wanted to steal all our bikes?"

That's when we heard the screams.

We ran over to the bike rack, where more kids were yelling. Only, the rack was practically empty, and most of the bikes were now riding away *on their own*!

They looked like runaway shopping carts rolling down the street. And *my* bike was there too!

Desmond and I took off chasing after the bikes, but they were fast.

"It's no use," said Desmond, who was breathing hard from running. "We'll never catch them on foot."

He ran back and found a little girl with a purple bike. It had handlebars with pink and purple tassels.

"Can I please borrow your bike and your helmet?" Desmond asked.

"Sure," the girl said.

Desmond hopped on the little bike. And that's when things got really weird!

CHAPTER NINE
DESMOND'S DARING RUN

As the bikes rode down the hill, Desmond chased after them. He pedaled so fast that the little bike wobbled from side to side.

I figured one thing out right away: Desmond Cole did not know how to ride a bike.

It was a good thing he had training wheels!

As he picked up speed, the pink and purple tassels blew in the breeze. I tried to run after him, but he was too fast.

I lost him after they reached the forest. It seemed like the stolen bikes were heading straight for the bike park on the other side.

What happened next? I couldn't tell you because I wasn't there.

But Desmond was. And this is what he told me:

Chasing after those bikes was the

scariest thing he'd ever done.

"STOP! PLEASE! STOP!" he yelled, holding on to the bike for dear life. He was going so fast that the training wheels started to smoke!

The bikes ahead of him turned onto a trail that led straight to the bike park. Desmond watched as the stolen bikes swerved and hopped over a fallen branch.

Then he remembered the bunny hop trick, so he tried it.

And it worked! That tiny bike made it over the branch! Desmond turned and followed the bikes, which were already at the start of the track.

By now, one thing was clear to Desmond. He was going to have to ride the racetrack!

He held his breath as he drove down the first hill. Clouds of dirt kicked up from the bikes. Desmond was covered in dust. He must have looked ridiculous, riding the track on a bike with training wheels and tassels! But if you were the only kid in town who knew how to investigate ghosts, then you probably got used to doing ridiculous things.

As he raced around the track, every bike in front of him fell over, one after another. Even with all the crashing, he kept his focus on the first stolen bike.

Which was my bike!

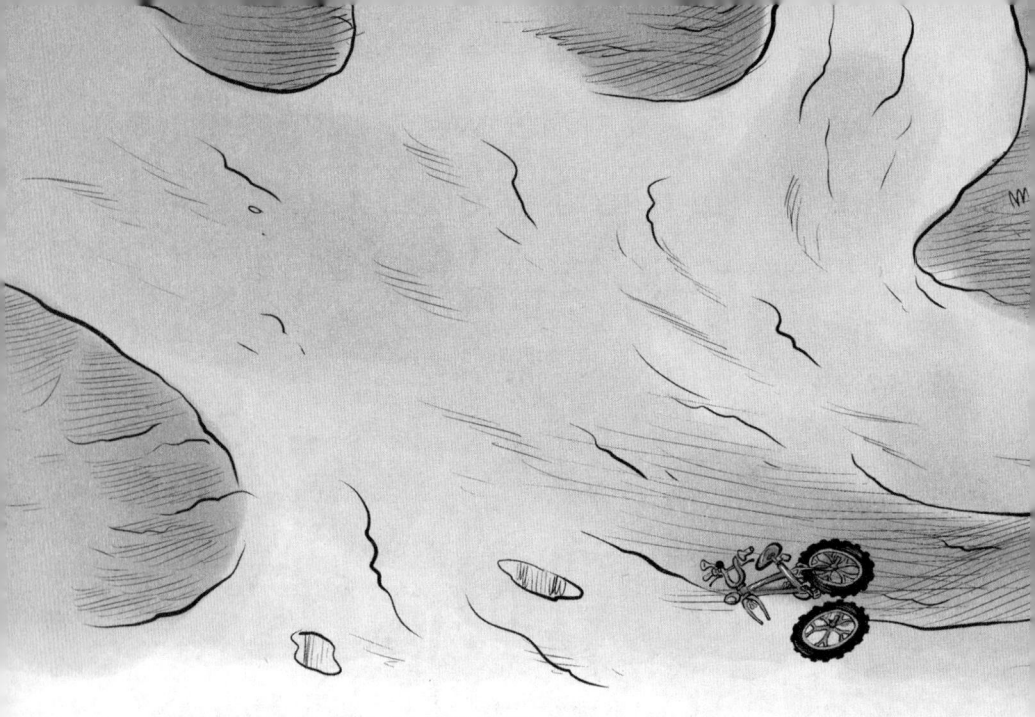

Desmond had almost reached my bike when it crashed. He tried to stop, but it was too late. Desmond was going up the Kicker.

His wheels blazed like a mini-rocket launched into orbit! The tassels on the handlebars fluttered like

tiny hands reaching for help. And Desmond . . . well, Desmond was screaming his head off.

There was no way Desmond could land the Kicker.

Desmond held on to the bike and prepared to hit the ground hard. But something froze him in midair. Desmond hovered above the ramp, and then he floated safely to the ground.

I might not have believed that part if I hadn't seen it with my own eyes.

When the other kids made it to the park, they started screaming. All their bikes were scattered on the track, totally destroyed. Mine, too. Broken frames, busted wheels—the place looked like a bike graveyard.

Then Kicker the ghost appeared. He had saved Desmond.

"I was hoping you would catch me," Desmond told Kicker.

"Happy to help," Kicker said.

I ran down to join them. "Kicker, did you steal our bikes?"

"It wasn't Kicker," said Desmond. "Will the real ghost thief please appear?"

With a bright shimmer, another ghost formed in front of us.

"Who are *you*?" Desmond asked.

"I'm Hal," he said. "I took your bikes."

All the kids started booing him.

"I was going to give them back," Hal said. "I only took the bikes that needed a tune-up."

Oh boy, I thought. *Another ghost who likes to fix things!*

Desmond quieted the crowd to let Hal explain himself.

The ghost took off his hat and put it over where his ghost heart might be. "You kids were riding on bikes with tires that need air, chains that are too tight, and handlebars that are too loose. It was driving me crazy! I had to do something to make it better."

Someone in the crowd yelled, "So what are we going to do now? All our bikes are ruined!"

Desmond and I looked at each other, because we had an idea that everyone would love.

CHAPTER TEN

Hal the Bike Healer

Here's a secret: Not all ghost secrets are bad.

I mean, take Hal for example. All he wants to do is fix broken bikes. Now that's exactly what he does! He fixed every single bike that day, even mine.

He does good work, too. In fact, he got rid of my dents and repainted the frame. I don't even need that electrical tape on the seat anymore. My bike is like new.

Hal is such a good mechanic that Desmond and I helped him set up his own repair shop at the bike park. He

gives free tune-ups, and he's right there to fix our bikes whenever we crash.

Oh, and as for Kicker, it turns out he's a great bike-riding instructor. Right now, he's working with one of his most challenging students ever: Desmond Cole.

At least whenever Desmond falls, Kicker is right there for him.

Maybe this Ghost Patrol thing is like riding a bike: Once you learn how to do it, you never forget.

DESMOND COLE GHOST PATROL

SURF'S UP, CREEPY STUFF!

CONTENTS

Chapter One: A Day at the Beach — 259

Chapter Two: YOU LOSE! — 267

Chapter Three: Dreary Beach — 281

Chapter Four: Haunted Sandcastles — 291

Chapter Five: Surf's Up, Creepy Stuff — 303

Chapter Six: Mersurfer Pop Up — 315

Chapter Seven: The Hot Dog Bird — 327

Chapter Eight: Totes Not Chill — 339

Chapter Nine: The Dune Octopus — 355

Chapter Ten: A Rad Day at the Beach — 369

CHAPTER ONE
A Day at the Beach

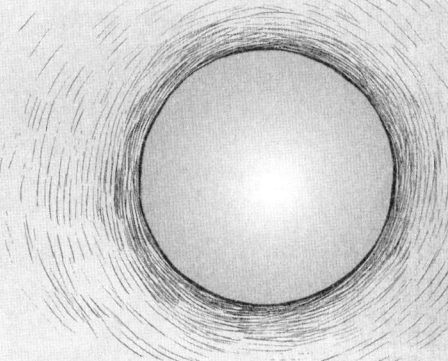

When people say something is "a day at the beach," they usually mean it was easy. Not me.

When I think about a day at the beach, I think about the hot sun burning the top of my head until I'm melting like a Popsicle.

I think about the sand burning the bottoms of my bare feet until I'm hopping around like a bunny. And I think about how sand gets everywhere: in my hair, in my shorts, even in my mouth. It's so gross!

I think about the birds and how they always want to eat everything you have. *Everything!* The last time I went to the beach, a bird tried to eat my swimsuit . . . and I was still wearing it! Talk about embarrassing!

A day at the beach also means dealing with the ocean. Ugh. Are there people who like spending a day getting salt water in their eyes? Not to mention how creepy the ocean is, with all that slimy seaweed and

jellyfish and *whatever else* is under there. And don't get me started on the crabs and sharks and squids.

Seriously, who would want to spend the day at the beach?

I'll tell you who: Desmond Cole. Of course, with Desmond, there's no chance a day at the beach will be easy. No chance at all!

CHAPTER TWO

YOU LOSE!

It all started on a sunny weekend morning.

I was playing my favorite video game, *Safety Zone*. If you haven't played it, this is what it's about: You are traveling through a strange world. The goal of the game is to stay away from danger and get to the safety zone . . . well, *safely*.

Of course, it's easy to get lost. Then you have to decide what to do.

Take a path in the dark forest? Nope. There's a *dragon* hiding there.

Take an easy shortcut over the old bridge? Oops. There's an *ogre* waiting on the other side.

That's why I always watch out for danger and never take any risks in the game. I just like to get to the safety zone in one piece.

Playing this game relaxed me.

But that day, the peaceful feeling didn't last long. Before I knew it, danger was knocking on my door.

It was Desmond Cole, my neigh-

bor and best friend. "My family is going to the beach," he told me. "Do you want to come with us?"

"Um, I was just playing my video game, and—"

"Oh no way, mister," my mom said. "It's so beautiful outside. You're not sitting in the house all day."

And just like that, the day I had planned was over. I had no choice. It was time to leave the *Safety Zone*. Because when my mom said "It's so beautiful outside," what she meant was *No more video games for you.*

I went upstairs and changed. Then my dad sprayed me with SPF 1,000, because you can never be too careful, right?

Desmond's parents were already outside packing the car. It was so crowded with stuff that it didn't look like there was any room left for us.

"Check this out," Desmond said, opening the door to the back seat. All I could see were huge floats everywhere. "It's a secret compartment," he said, and he crawled underneath the beach junk.

I followed him, and sure enough, Desmond had made himself a little cove. It was pretty comfy in there too.

"How far away is the beach?" I asked him. It was my first time going since I moved to Kersville.

"It's not too far," Desmond said. "You're going to love Dreary Beach. It has the softest sand, the warmest water, and the biggest waves!"

Dreary Beach? Didn't "dreary" mean "dull and boring"? What kind of name was that for a beach?

Before I could ask, Zax floated into the car. He was the ghost that lived with me, but he wasn't scary. He was just kind of annoying like a little brother. "Wow!" he said. "You're going to Dreary Beach! Do you have room for a ghost?"

Do you have room for a ghost? A question like that used to scare me, but not anymore. Not when it came to a ghost like Zax.

"I'm sorry, Zax," Desmond said. "Take a look around. There's barely room for Andres and me! Plus, my

parents are cool, but they're not, like, ghosts-in-the-car cool. Maybe next time, okay?"

Zax nodded. "I get it. Have fun surfing. Hang ten, dudes!"

As soon as Zax was gone, I asked Desmond, "So, does that mean we're going to a dull, boring beach with no ghosts?"

"I guess," Desmond said.

Now Dreary Beach sounded like it was going to be perfect. The only problem was that there weren't many dull and boring places in Kersville. I had learned that the hard way.

CHAPTER THREE
DREARY BEACH

"That's weird," Desmond's mom said when we arrived at Dreary Beach.

Weird? That wasn't what I wanted to hear. My heart started pounding. I poked my head out from under the floats and looked out the window.

The parking lot was practically empty, and when I looked at the ocean, there weren't a lot of people.

"I don't understand," Mrs. Cole said. "I thought it would be crowded on a beautiful day like this."

Cool! I thought. It was almost like having the beach all to ourselves. What could be better than that?

I couldn't believe how much stuff the Coles had packed. There was a tent, a solar-powered generator, a wagon, a table, a computer, rafts, coolers, chairs, speakers, floats, buckets, shovels, towels, fans, sunscreen, and even a minifridge! Don't ask me how they fit all of it into their car, but they did.

And we had to carry everything down the long wooden walkway that went over a set of sand dunes. "They don't want anyone walking on these dunes," Desmond said. "They want to protect the wildlife living here."

I swallowed, worried. "How wild?" I asked. I needed to know what to expect. Was there a giant octopus waiting to grab us in its slippery arms? Were there *land sharks*?

My eyes opened wide as I looked around.

Desmond laughed. "Calm down, Andres," he said. "I was just talking about wildlife like birds and deer and turtles. There's nothing to worry about."

I let out a sigh of relief. Once again, my mind was running wild. But can you blame me? This is Kersville, after all.

Since the beach was pretty empty, we had no trouble finding the perfect spot. And that was when the Coles got to work setting up everything they brought. Before I knew it, they had built a tent with all the comforts of home.

I looked around the beach. There were a few other families on the sand and surfers riding the waves. *Too bad Zax couldn't come*, I thought. *He would have loved this.*

"What should we do first?" I asked Desmond.

He held up a bucket and shovel. "I challenge you to a haunted sandcastle building contest!"

CHAPTER FOUR

Haunted Sandcastles

Let me tell you, the Dreary Beach sand is the best sandcastle-building sand in the whole wide world. First of all, it's not hot. It doesn't burn your feet. In fact, it feels nice and cool when you touch it.

Not only that, but the sand on

Dreary Beach really sticks together. Desmond brought tons of buckets, and no matter which he used, the sand always stayed in the shape. Even the crazy shapes worked.

In fact, the sand was so perfect that Desmond and I were building the two biggest sandcastles ever in no time flat. They were so big that we could almost fit inside them.

Other kids on the beach gathered around to watch us work. "What are you guys building?" one girl asked.

Desmond tried to hide a sly smile. "Haunted sandcastles."

"No, you're not," the girl said, and some of the other kids shook their heads. Nobody believed us. But they stayed and watched as we finished.

When I put the flag on my last guard post, the kids actually started applauding.

"Are your castles really haunted?" a boy asked.

"No," I answered. "But if they were, they would be haunted by the, um, *ocean ghost*." It was the only thing I could think of.

"For real?" the boy asked.

"Yeah," I said. "The ocean ghost travels around from one sandcastle to the other, searching for its perfect home."

Desmond smiled and added, "And if you're not careful, it might go home with *you!*"

The boy's eyes widened, but some of the other kids tried to laugh. It was a worried laugh, though. Desmond's face looked so serious that I started to feel a little nervous too. And I was the one who had made up the ocean ghost.

"Don't believe me?" Desmond asked the kids. "If you want to see the ocean ghost, do this: Look at the water and say, 'Ocean ghost, ocean ghost, let me see you. Ocean ghost, ocean ghost, let me free you.'"

Some of the kids laughed again, but one of the girls turned around to face the sea and said,  "Ocean ghost, ocean ghost, let me see you. Ocean ghost, ocean ghost, let me free you."

And that's when it happened! A real ghost popped out of Desmond's sandcastle!

The kids ran screaming down the beach. Even from far away, I still heard one high-pitched scream. Then I realized it was coming from *me*!

Desmond laughed so hard that he fell down. The ghost from the castle was none other than Zax.

He looked at me with the saddest eyes. "I'm sorry, Andres. Desmond thought this would be a very funny prank, and it *was*, right?"

I couldn't answer him right then. My heart was too busy trying to get back to its normal speed. Not that it ever would.

CHAPTER FIVE
SURF'S UP, CREEPY STUFF

"I can't believe you would scare me like that!" I yelled at Zax. "I thought you were my friend! And how did you get here? You couldn't fit in the car."

Zax smirked. "I'm a ghost. I can fit anywhere. Watch this."

He flew over to the teeniest-tiniest

shell and shrank himself right into it. Then he popped back out. "Pretty cool, right?"

I nodded because it was.

"Sorry, Andres," he said again. "Why don't we go surf? Check out those waves!"

"And look how much fun those surfers are having," Desmond said.

They did look like they were having a great time. Then I smiled. I didn't come here to be mad, and it wasn't too late to make this beach day super fun.

We all ran back to Desmond's tent. Well, Zax didn't run. He just kind of floated. While they grabbed a surfboard and a bodyboard, I took a big pineapple-shaped float.

On the way out, I noticed some birds on top of the tent. "What are they doing up there?" I asked Desmond.

"I don't know," he said. "They're probably looking for food. Too bad my mom is cooking. They never eat anything she makes."

Zax gagged a little bit. He tried Mrs. Cole's lasagna once. It was unforgettable . . . in a bad way!

We raced down to the water and splashed our way in. Just like the sand, the water was perfect. And I didn't feel any of the slimy things around my ankles. I was really loving Dreary Beach.

Zax jumped on the surfboard, and he caught a wave right away. I don't know how, but he was an excellent surfer!

Desmond caught the next wave on his bodyboard and rode it all the way in. It looked like so much fun.

I waited for the next perfect wave with my pineapple-shaped float. Riding the waves looked scary, but I wanted to try it.

Then some of the other surfers floated over to me. I waved hello, and they waved back. But as they got closer, I knew something really weird was going on.

Their hands were webbed.

Webbed!

I figured they were wearing a new kind of surfing outfit, but then one of them leaped out of the water. He had green skin, a fishy face, and sharp teeth!

I paddled on my float and swam away. I could hear them hiss behind me. Then a creature reached out and unplugged my float.

The air zizzed out of my pineapple so fast, I went flying into the air. I flew so high and so far that I crashed right into my perfect haunted sandcastle, flattening it out.

Great, I thought, trying to catch my breath. *Now I have sand in my swimsuit* and *monsters in my ocean.*

CHAPTER SIX
MERSURFER POP UP

Before I could stand up, Desmond and Zax came sailing through the air to join me. They crashed into Desmond's haunted sandcastle.

As Desmond sat there, I asked him, "Did you see those surfers? They're monsters!"

Zax shook his ghost head. "No, they're not monsters. They're mer-surfers."

"Mersurfers?" Desmond and I repeated.

Zax planted his surfboard into the

sand and filled us in on everything he knew about these creatures. He told us that mersurfers lived in the deepest, darkest part of the ocean and that they only came out on perfect beach days.

"Like today!" I said.

Zax nodded. "That's right, but listen. Mersurfers hate sharing the beach. They try to chase everybody away."

"That's not nice," Desmond said. "Dreary Beach is supposed to be for everyone. There's no way I'm leaving."

Zax looked at us, worried. "We have to pack up our stuff and go home right now," he said. "They might come ashore."

Thinking about that made my heart slip into my stomach.

Just then a giant wave crashed, splashing over Desmond and me. When I opened my eyes, there was a mersurfer standing right next to us. He raised his green slimy arms, and the next thing we knew he was chasing us and the other kids down the beach.

All the families and people sunbathing scattered, screaming. But when we passed the Cole's tent, his parents were inside dancing to their beach music. They had no idea what was going on!

We kept running, making it all the way up to the pier. That was when the mersurfer stopped chasing us. He turned around and went back toward his buddies in the water.

On the pier, Desmond and I tried to catch our breath. Even Zax was breathing hard, and he's a ghost!

"That was crazy!" I said, panting like a dog.

"I know," Desmond agreed. "Scaring people at the beach isn't right."

I raised one eyebrow. "Really? You guys scared *me* at the beach."

"That's different," Desmond said. "We're your friends. These monsters are up to no good. And we are not going to let them take Dreary Beach away from us."

We. I knew Desmond was talking about the Ghost Patrol.

It was official. The battle for the beach was on!

CHAPTER SEVEN

THE HOT DOG BIRD

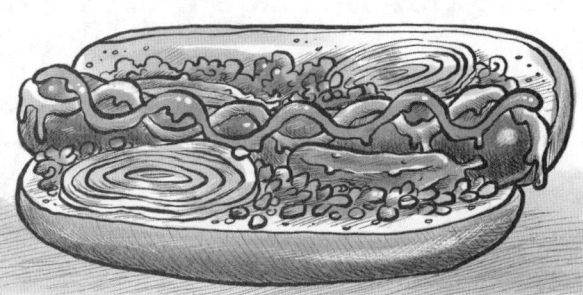

"First things first," Desmond said. "We need to eat."

I followed him over to a hot dog stand. How could he be thinking about food at a time like this? We were just chased off the beach by a mersurfer of all things!

Then he handed me a hot dog, and my stomach did a happy dance. I guess fear makes me hungry!

We ate our hot dogs as we walked down the pier. Desmond Cole always had a plan, and this time, I started to

figure out what he was thinking. The pier stretched over the water, and from there, we could see the whole beach and the ocean . . . including the mersurfers.

Most of the creatures were in the waves, shredding on their surfboards. A few other mersurfers were scaring people away. It was something crazy to see. Whenever the people ran away, they totally ended up scaring the birds.

The weird thing was that the mersurfers were only bothering people at one part of the beach. Other people in other places were left alone to swim and have fun.

"That area must be the best surfing spot," Zax said.

We kept walking toward the end of the pier where people were fishing. Some birds sat on the handrails, squawking. It almost sounded like they were talking to one another.

I was about to take a bite of my hot dog when one of those birds swooped down and stole it right out of my hands! "Hey!" I screamed. "That's mine!"

I tried to swat it away, but another bird swooped down and grabbed my hair. "Aaaargh!" I screamed.

Sand in my shorts, monsters on the beach. And now birds in my hair. I'd had enough of this beach day.

Suddenly the strangest thing happened. All the birds flew away. Then every single fishing pole yanked forward, like each one had caught a fish at the same time.

But the fishers weren't excited. They looked over into the water, screamed, and ran away.

What now? I thought.

A second later, I saw it. Mersurfers were climbing up the fishing lines and onto the pier. Everyone ran—fast!

A bird landed on the handrail. Yes, it was the same one that had stolen my hot dog and held it in its little beak. The mersurfers surrounded that bird and tried to scare it, but it wasn't going anywhere. It was too busy eating.

When it was done, the hot dog

bird flapped its wings, and all the mersurfers freaked out. Like surfers jumping from a bad wave, those sea monsters totally bailed!

I looked at Desmond. He had his thinking face on. I could tell that he was putting some mersurfer-size puzzle pieces together.

CHAPTER EIGHT

TOTES NOT CHILL

A few minutes later, Desmond and I were back in his parents' mega-tent. Desmond searched through a set of drawers. "Those mersurfers are up to something," he said, pulling out big colorful beach towels. "I don't think it's just about surfing the waves."

"What do you mean?" I asked.

"I mean, why would they scare people away from the pier if all they wanted was a place to surf?" he asked.

"Maybe they just want to be left alone," I suggested.

Desmond shook his head. "Then why haven't they scared everyone from the rest of the beach? Why didn't they scare my parents?"

I didn't have an answer, but how was I supposed to understand a bunch of mersurfers?

Desmond closed the drawer. "I think they're trying to keep us from something. This tent is too far away from whatever it is, so they're leaving us alone."

"Maybe we should stay here then, where it's safe," I said.

But I knew what Desmond was going to say before he even said it. "The Ghost Patrol needs to figure out what those mersurfers are up to." Then he threw a beach towel in my direction. "Follow me."

The plan was simple. And a little nuts! Zax shrank down, tucked himself into a shell, and hopped along the sand. He was our lookout.

As for Desmond and me, we were lying on the sand with our beach towels spread out on top of us.

It was all about camouflage. Most of the mersurfers were in the water, so Desmond and I just looked like beach towels. And there were a lot of other towels left behind on the sand, thanks to those creatures.

A small group of mersurfers gathered on the beach. When they weren't looking, Zax would let us know it was safe to sneak closer to them. If one of the mersurfers was going to turn around, Zax would signal us again, and back under the towels we'd go.

Ugh! It will take days or even weeks to get all the sand off me! I thought.

Once we were finally close enough to the mersurfers, we could hear them talking.

"This evening, when the sun is low," one of them said. "That's when we strike."

I held my breath. *They were making a plan—but a plan for what?*

As I inched a little closer to hear them, a huge gust of wind howled. The breeze kicked up my towel and blew it away.

If you don't like having sand in your shorts, then you will definitely not like having sand in your shorts while looking up at a bunch of mer-surfers. It was a nightmare!

Then one of them spoke to me, but it didn't hiss or growl. It sounded kind of . . . cool. "Yo, little dude. It's, like, totes not chill to sneak up on other dudes, dude!"

I stared at the mersurfer. I didn't know what to say because it was right.

The others bared their teeth at me. They were trying to scare me, but it wasn't going to work this time.

I remembered that hot dog bird on the pier. It made those mersurfers run away just by being a bird.

I didn't have any wings to flap, so I did the next best thing.

CAAAAWWWW!

It was my best crow noise, and let me tell you, it worked. If you ever find yourself surrounded by a group

of mersurfers, all you have to do is flap your arms and caw like a crow.

Those monsters bolted faster than lightning!

Desmond saw the whole thing. "Hmm," he said. "It looks like we're going to need a new plan."

CHAPTER NINE
THE DUNE OCTOPUS

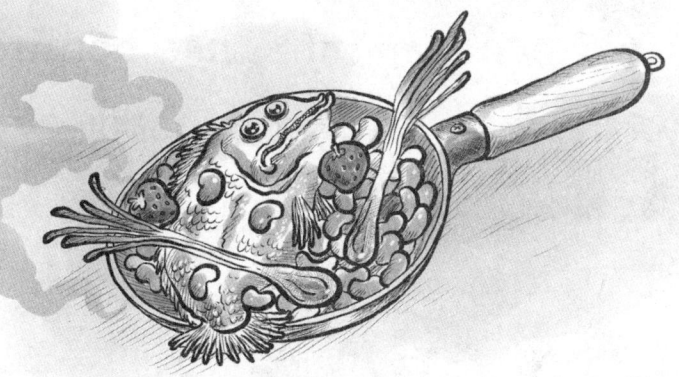

Back at the Coles' beach tent, something smelled . . . fishy. It wasn't the mersurfers this time. Desmond's mom was cooking.

We held our noses tight and ran upstairs. (Yes, the tent actually had an upstairs!) We peeked out the plastic window with binoculars. The mersurfers had come back, and they were making a bonfire.

"If we can get into that bonfire party, then we can stop their evil plan," said Desmond.

I gulped a loud gulp. "Maybe we should just let them enjoy their evil plan and go home?"

Nothing was going to get me out there again. Well, almost nothing.

"Boys! Dinner is ready!" It was Mrs. Cole calling from downstairs.

This time my stomach gurgled a loud gurgle. "Like I was saying, let's catch some mersurfers... and maybe skip dinner."

Desmond nodded and yelled, "Thanks, Mom. Can we get our food to go? We want to eat on the beach."

Then he turned to me and asked, "Have you ever been scuba diving?

Desmond and I held our bags of food as we walked across the sand in wetsuits. The suits really made us look like the mersurfers.

Zax flew next to us. "Are you sure this is going to work?"

"No," Desmond said. "But I'm running out of ideas."

We got to the bonfire and tried to blend in. And guess what? It worked! Nobody noticed two kids and a

ghost. Instead, most of the mersurfers were focused on clearing a path in the sand.

That was when I felt a tap on my shoulder. "Okay, dudes, like, follow me," the mersurfer said. "The little ones are going to make a break for it soon. We need to make sure the dunes are bird-free. You dig?"

I didn't dig. I had no idea what he was talking about! But still, I said, "Totally, um, dude."

The creature smiled. "Radical, little human dude."

Our secret was out! Oh, who were we fooling? We didn't look anything like mersurfers in these wetsuits. Zax, Desmond, and I were busted!

Then the mersurfer put its arms around Desmond and me. "Relax. It's cool, little human dudes and ghost bud. We could use your help."

It took us to the dunes where the wildlife lived. Then it pointed toward some tall grass and the sand started moving like something was under it.

I totally freaked out. Because I knew exactly what was hiding in the ground: *a giant dune octopus!*

CHAPTER TEN

A Rad Day at the Beach

Desmond grabbed hold of me. "Chill out and look."

Slowly, a bunch of tiny crawly things climbed out of the sand. And they weren't dune octopus tentacles. They were baby turtles!

I couldn't believe my eyes.

Lots of baby turtles were hatching. They were about to crawl to the ocean for the first time.

"Listen, little human dudes," the mersurfer said. "I know you two are the same ones who built those great sandcastles earlier. Sorry we had to wreck them, but they were in the turtles' path."

Now it all made sense! The mersurfers were guarding the baby sea turtles. They wanted to make sure the babies made it to the water safely.

"We aren't evil, I promise," the mersurfer continued. "We don't have anything against people. But birds are another story." It shivered.

Desmond snapped his fingers. "Aha! Mersurfers are scared of birds. So when you scared us and we ran away, we scared the birds."

"Exactly!" said the mersurfer as he relaxed. "We needed to make sure these little turtle dudes make it to the ocean safe and sound."

Desmond smiled. "Don't worry. Andres and I can help."

And we did. As the baby sea turtles made their way from the dunes, Desmond and I started throwing little pieces of his mom's food at the curious birds. As soon as they smelled it, those birds turned green and flew off. Pretty soon, they all stayed far away from the food *and* the turtles.

Desmond, Zax, and I watched as the baby turtles waded into their new ocean home. Then we cheered. It was the best *beach day* ever!

Turns out, Dreary Beach is not so dreary after all. Actually, there's no better beach.

Desmond, Zax, and I go back whenever we can. We are getting a lot better at surfing, though I'm sure that's because the mersurfers are great teachers.

The only gross thing is that the mersurfers actually love Desmond's mom's cooking. Sushi macaroni, tuna-fish ice cream, olive–peanut butter surprise—you name it, they love it. It makes no sense at all, but I'm glad his mom's food makes them happy.

As for me, I guess you can say I changed too. Now I know that a day at Dreary Beach can be . . . as the mersurfers say, rad!

Here's a peek at
DESMOND COLE GHOST PATROL'S
next big case!

Everybody loves the zoo, right? Hey, who doesn't like cool animals? Who doesn't want to spend the day hanging out with lions, tigers, bears, and snakes? Okay, *maybe* not the snakes. They make my skin crawl.

An excerpt from **Night of the Zombie Zookeeper**

But the rest of the zoo? Believe it or not, I'm just like every other kid. I love zoos!

I mean, where else can you see animals from all over the world in one place . . . *up close*?

Not to mention the merry-go-round, ice-cream stands, and a train that goes all the way around the park. Want to get from the apes to the petting farm without standing up? Then all aboard the Zoo Choo Train!

Zoos even have the coolest gift shops.

An excerpt from **Night of the Zombie Zookeeper**